TO BE Maya

Claudia Recinos Seldeen

An imprint of Enslow Publishing

WEST 44 BOOKS™

Please visit our website, www.west44books.com.
For a free color catalog of all our high-quality
books, call toll free 1-800-398-2504.

Cataloging-in-Publication Data

Names: Recinos Seldeen, Claudia.
Title: To be Maya / Claudia Recinos Seldeen.
Description: New York : West 44, 2023. | Series: West 44 YA
verse
Identifiers: ISBN 9781978596191 (pbk.) | ISBN 9781978596184
(library bound) | ISBN 9781978596207 (ebook)
Subjects: LCSH: American poetry--21st century. | Poetry,
Modern--21st century. | English poetry.
Classification: LCC PS584.R435 2023 | DDC 811'.6--dc23

First Edition

Published in 2023 by
Enslow Publishing LLC
29 East 21st Street
New York, NY 10011

Editor: Caitie McAneney
Designer: Katelyn E. Reynolds

Photo Credits: Cvr, p. 1 (lockers) ND700/Shutterstock.com;
cvr, p.1 (stripe pattern) Mykola Mazuryk/Shutterstock.com;
cvr, pp. 1–191 (circles) oculo/Shutterstock.com.

Printed in the United States of America

CPSIA compliance information: Batch #CS23W44: For further information contact
Enslow Publishing LLC, New York, New York at 1-800-398-2504.

For anyone who's ever felt out of place
or misunderstood. And for Ken and
Brandon, my very own marbles.

What It Means to Be Maya

The Mayan people once lived
all
     over
          Central America.

They built temples
     out of stone.

They made knives
     out of flint.

They made jewelry
     out of jade.

They carved their life
     out of the jungle.

They were fierce and proud.

My mother named me Maya
to connect me
     to my past.

And to Guatemala.
  The country where she was born.
  The country she left
  five years
  before I came along.

She named me Maya
for the Mayan people,
our ancestors.

But I am not fierce.
I am not stone
  or flint
  or jade.

I am just a girl.
And my name is my own.

Are You Excited?

Are you excited
    for tomorrow?
        Gemma asks.

We're lying
on the grass.
Still out of breath
from our run
through the sprinklers.

The sun
is shining
like a diamond.
Its heat
fills my lungs
and stings my skin.

I bite my lip
to keep the wrong words
from
      tumbling
           out.

I don't want to tell
my best friend
that I'm excited
    to be a sophomore.

To see
      what a new year
            will bring.

I'm excited!

But,
I don't want
to tell her
because
      she's going to miss
         all of it.

So, I just shrug.
I close my eyes
and draw
a quick sketch
of us in my head.
      Two girls lying
      so close
      our fingers
      touch.

I open my eyes
and ask,
Are you *excited?*

Gemma's shrug
is an echo
of my own.

I'm worried
everyone
will hate me,
she says.

I nod
because I understand.

Because I'll be going
to the same school
as last year.
I'll be seeing
all the same faces.
But Gemma will be
         across town
                  at the private school.

Gemma will be on her own.

Niñas Lindas

Footsteps
c r u n c h
on the grass.
Gemma's mother
stands
over
us,
blotting out the sun.

Niñas lindas,
she calls us.
Pretty girls.

Her Cuban accent
makes me think
of an orange,
brazen
and bold
and syrup sweet.

She holds
a bottle of sunscreen
out to Gemma.
When we were kids,
Gemma and I
would sometimes
fall asleep
on the grass.

We would wake up
h o u r s
later.
Gemma
would be
flushed pink.
The sun turned
her skin
the color of
s t r a w b e r r i e s.

But I
only ever turned
brown.
Like coffee
with not enough
milk.

Gemma's mother
waits
while my friend
smears the lotion
on her freckled nose.

But
when she turns to me
her brows
come together
in a loose
knot.

You're okay,
she says.
You're not as
delicate and fair
as Gemma.

Her words
stay on the lawn
long after she's gone.

Her words
hang in the air
like paper wasps.

Her words
settle
like the sun's stinging rays
on my heart.

My Mother

I could ride my bike
home from Gemma's.
But my mother always
picks me up.

It's not safe,
she tells me each time I complain.
You're too young.

Todo en su tiempo.
Everything in its time.

When my mother picks me up,
she doesn't wait in the car
like most mothers do.

She knocks
on the door.

She rings
the doorbell.

She comes
inside.

Giving Thanks

Here
is a secret
that's not
really
a secret:
My mother
cleans
Gemma's house.

It's because of
my mother
that the coffee table
is dust free.
That the floor
shines
like a mirror.
That I know
Gemma
at all.

My mother cleans
a lot
of houses,
but none of them
are as big
as Gemma's.

My mother
waits for me
by the door.
Still wearing her
crisp white uniform.
Her smile
crinkles the corners of her eyes
like tissue paper.

She thanks
Gemma's mother
again
for having me over.

Like I haven't already said
gracias
a hundred times.

Like I haven't been
hanging out at Gemma's
almost every day
since I was eight.

Like my mother
hasn't worked all day
cleaning this house.

Gemma's Desk

Andres sits next to me
in homeroom.
He takes the desk
that should've been
Gemma's.

Andres is
my oldest friend,
besides Gemma.
Sometimes
when I look at him,
I think
of my tenth birthday party.
I think of how he ate
all the frosting flowers
off my cake.

But today
I only see
that he's sitting at
Gemma's desk.
And he's not
Gemma.

Andres

Andres's father
is from Peru.
His mother
is from Mexico.

Andres likes to brag
about being
from two
different countries.
Each
has its own customs
and traditions.

But when he has to
fill out forms
for school,
he has to check
Latino.
Just like Gemma and me.

Marbles

When we
      were kids,
we were
      like
a bag
      of marbles.

We were all
      jumbled
together.

But
as we
got
older,
      we
      sorted
      ourselves
      into groups.

Andres
and Gemma
and I
are in
the
same
group.

But now
Gemma
is gone,
and we are down
to two marbles.

New Friends

Andres leans
across the aisle.
He raises
one dark eyebrow.

*Do you think
Gemma
has made any
new friends?*
he asks.

In my head,
there's a
mental drawing
of Gemma,
her nose turned pink
by the sun.

I look
at the drawing
and shake
my head.

*None
as cool as us,*

I say.

Laughter

The laughter
behind me
is a soft huff
of air.
I turn my head.
Josh Williams
is leaning back
in his seat.
Laughing.

He's wearing his
lacrosse jersey.
I think of how,
as kids,
we used to play
kickball together.
But now
he plays lacrosse
with Brian Davis,
whose house
my mother
cleans.

Is something funny?
I snap.

For a moment,
there's only silence.

17

Then Josh's smile
w i d e n s.
He throws
his hands
up
like he's
warding off a tiger.

If I say no,
he says,
will you let me live?

Josh's teeth
are model straight
from years of braces.
But his grin
      is
              lopsided.

I think of how
my mother
told me, once,
that things that are
      different
are sometimes
      more beautiful
      because of
      their differences.

I turn around.

My anger
      runs
            out of me
            like water
            through a drain.

When we were kids,
      we were marbles,
bouncing happily
      off one another.

But over the years
we've arranged
ourselves
      into neat
      little groups.

And Josh Williams
      and
            I
aren't in
      the same group.

Hailey Miller

Metal lockers
c l a n g
and
s l a m.

Voices
   b
  u
    z
    z
like
   swarming
bees.

Laughter
      rings
          out
     like
a bell.

I twist
and spin
the lock.
     I count
     the turns
     out loud.

But my locker
refuses
to open.

And,
next to me,
I hear
the impatient
clack
of Hailey Miller's
pink nails.
Like the
tickticktick
of a pilot light
before the gas
catches fire.

She lets out
an angry sigh
that could be
the twin sister
of my own.

Then she whispers.
        (Too quietly
        to be meant
        for me.
        Too loud
        to not be
        overheard).

We're not picking tomatoes
in a field.
We don't have
all day.

All the words
I could say—

I don't work
        on a farm.
I was born here,
        just like you.
I am
        just
                like
                        you—
drift
out
of my head
like
smoke.

Because
when I turn
around,
I see
Hailey and her friends.
They look like feathered swans,
long and lean,
in their summer dresses.
Niñas lindas.

22

Pretty girls ...

They stare at me.
They stare at me.
They stare at me.

As I
bump
and stumble
out of their way.
As I wheel away
from the sound
of their laughter.

The Only Time I Can Breathe

In art class,
I let go.

Streaks of red
for the anger
burning inside me.

Flecks of blue
for the sadness
that hovers
at the
edges.

The paper
wrinkles and softens.

The watercolors
bleed
into one another
like tears.

I pull another
sheet of paper out.

I draw
a girl,
her pink face
turned up
to catch the sun.

Gemma ...

But
when I bring
paintbrush
to paper
and try to add myself
to the picture,
I realize
I don't know
how.

So,
I just leave
a blank space
where
the second girl
should be.

The Way Things Are

At school,
it has
always been
Gemma and Andres and me.
Like
three points
on a triangle.

But now
there's only
me and Andres.

We sit together
on the grass
in front of the school.

Andres and me.
And our lunch,
spread
on the ground
between us.

Simple

Andres's face
is soft and distant.
His eyes
are on
Brian Davis,
who's throwing
a football
in the air
several feet away.

Sometimes I wish,
Andres says,
everything
was as simple
as football.

In my mind,
I see marbles.
I see them lined up
in neat
little
rows.

Things are
exactly
that
simple,
I say.

Andres sighs.
Maybe for you,
he says.

And then he closes
his eyes and says
nothing more.

Spinning

I'm walking
toward the buses.

I'm cutting across
the lawn
in front of the school.

I'm glad
the day is over.

And that's when the stitching
on my
backpack
r i p s.
That's when my
books
          waterfall
                    out.

My face
grows hot
as people
weave
around me.

My skin
crawls
with the sound
of their
laughter.

Frustrated tears
glass
my eyes.
It takes me
a minute
to realize
Josh Williams
is kneeling beside me.
Picking my pencils
off the ground
like he's
plucking flowers.

For a minute
(just a minute)
I am grateful.

But then
his brows
come together.
He says,
What's this?

I look down.

I see
he's holding
my sketchbook.
My heart
tightens
like a fist.

I snatch my book
away.
Josh looks up,
gray eyes
blinking.

We stay
like that
a while.

And when
I finally stand up,
all the blood
rushes
from my head
and the world
spins
in a slow circle.

To Dive or Not to Dive

There's a scar
over Josh's
left eyebrow.
There's
a freckle
on his chin.
It reminds me
of a stray
pencil mark.

He asks
why I have
so many books.

I think of
my broken locker.
I think of Hailey Miller's laughter,
sharp as knives.

My lips
pinch shut.

But Josh fills
the empty space
with a story
about lacrosse camp.

He tells me
how he had to carry
so much
gear.
How it made him
want to
quit.
But I know he never did.

The way
his sentences
trip
over
each
other
makes me think of
fireflies
          dancing
                    in the summer sky.

I tip my head
to one side.
I wonder
what it would be like
to draw him.
Streaks of gold.
Dabs of white.
Two gray eyes
like the sky
in winter.
Or the blades
in Hailey Miller's
laughter.

33

Or the deep end
of the ocean
that your mother warns you
is too dangerous
to swim in.
But which you
long
to dive into
anyway.

A Letter

There's an envelope
sitting
on the kitchen table.
A crisp
white
rectangle
floating on
a wooden sea.

I can tell
by the handwriting
that the envelope
is from Guatemala.
But
the return address
isn't one I recognize.
Even though
the envelope
is addressed
to me.

I pick
the envelope
up.
I hold it
in my hands.

The letters
I get
from my aunt—
my mother's
only sister—
are thick
and heavy.
They are filled with news
and gossip
about relatives
I've never met.

But
this letter
is thin.
This letter is like a flower petal.
I hold it
very
carefully.

It's from your grandmother,
my mother tells me.

I frown
because
her mother died
when I was still
a baby.

But then she says,
It's from your father's mother.

36

The sound
of her footsteps
as she walks away
is an echo
of my own
startled heartbeat.

Querida Maya

Querida Maya,
the letter says.
Dear Maya.

My father
and my mother
came here from Guatemala
years
before I was born.

My mother came
against her family's
wishes.
She chose
my father
over them.
It made her
an outsider.

But my mother
has never told me
what happened
after that.

I've never met my father.
I've never spoken to him.
I know he's alive.

But I know
I'm not dear to him.
I'm not *querida Maya.*
If I had been,
he wouldn't have
left us.
He would
have
stayed.

Querida Maya,
my grandmother's letter
says.

I put
the letter
down.
I wonder
how I could be dear
to someone
I've never even met.

I think of
my mother
all alone
in a foreign country.
I think of
my father,
whose face
I don't even know.

I look
at the piece of paper
in my hand.
At the handwriting
I don't recognize.
At the words
that have come
too late.

I crumple
my grandmother's letter
up
without reading it.

I walk
across the kitchen.

I
throw
the
letter
away.

Telephone

If I had
my own phone,
like any
normal teenager,
I could lock myself
in my room
and text Gemma.

But my mother says
only people
with secrets
need their own phone.
And mothers
and daughters
shouldn't have secrets.

If This Were a Movie

I sit
on the kitchen floor,
the clunky house phone
in my lap.
My fingers
dance
over the keypad.
They pick out
Gemma's number.
Like they have
a thousand times over.

I don't
even wait
for Gemma
to finish saying hello.
I launch
into my tale of
ripped backpacks.
Gray eyes.
Crooked smiles.

If this were a movie,
Gemma says,
this is where
you'd fall in love.

I open my mouth
to say something
clever.
But nothing comes out
except a sigh of relief.

I realize I'm glad
this isn't a movie.
Because I've never seen
a movie like this.
A movie where a girl
who looks like me
ends up
with someone like
Josh Williams.

Todo en Su Tiempo

My mother
cups my face
in her hands.

Her hands
are dry
like newspaper.
But
they are also
whisper
soft.

You're too young, she says,
to be thinking about boys.
To be giving your heart away.
To be spinning fantasies.

It's not safe, she says,
to be so open.
To be so careless.
To be so free with your heart.

Todo en su tiempo.
Everything in its time.

But shouldn't I have a say
in when the time is right?

Tortillas

Guatemalan tortillas
aren't like
Mexican tortillas,
white and floury.

Guatemalan tortillas
are fluffier.
Doughier.
They're shaped
into flat discs
between hands
that turn
and clap.
Quick quick!
Like dancing.
Like a heartbeat:
clapclapclap.

When I was little,
I used to make
tortillas
with my mom.
But it's been
a long time
since then.
My hands
have lost
their rhythm.

Breakfast

My mom
always
leaves tortillas
and *frijoles volteados*
on the stovetop
for breakfast.
Refried black beans
as thick as
peanut butter.
Salty
and garlicky
and oniony.

The smell makes
my mouth water.

But, today,
I think of how
the garlic
stays
on my tongue.
Even after
I brush my teeth.

Today,
I pour myself
a bowl of cereal
and cold milk.

I leave the
tortillas
and
frijoles volteados
on the stove.

Homeroom

There's a moment,
right before
I walk into homeroom,
when I forget
Gemma is gone.

My heart
f i z z e s
and
p o p s
with excitement.

But then
I walk in.
I see Andres sitting
where Gemma
used to be.
And my heart
goes quiet.

Josh is nowhere
to be found.
I'm troubled
by the way
my stomach
        dips
with disappointment.

But even more troubling
is the way
my heart
l i f t s
when he finally walks
into the room.

Frida Kahlo

The air stirs
behind me
as Josh settles
into his desk.

What's up,
Frida Kahlo?
he asks.

Frida Kahlo
was a Mexican painter.
Being compared
to her
makes my heart
      secretly
            sing.

I smile at Josh
over my shoulder.
And when I turn
back around,
I pretend I can't see
Andres raising
one dark eyebrow.

Late

Between classes,
I take the long way
to my locker.
I drag my feet.
I weave
through the
halls.

Hailey Miller
is gone
by the time
I get there.

I celebrate
with a quiet grin.

When my locker
gets stuck,
there's no
barbed wire sting
of laughter.
No half-whispered
put-downs.
No impatient
sighs.

51

I can close my eyes.
I can breathe.
I can go slow.

But after four tries,
my locker still won't open.

The sound
of my own heartbeat
reminds me of the
clack clack clack
of Hailey's nails.

I tell myself
to calm down.
I tell myself
to try again.
But the shrill scream
of the bell
rips
through the halls,
telling me
I'm late for gym.

Tar-Day

My gym teacher's face
is always red
like he's holding his breath.
Even though he's always letting it out
in a firecracker burst of shouts.

Tardy!
he snaps at me
when I walk in.

Then his lip curls.
Tar-day!

The jolt of understanding
is like a crack of electricity.
I realize
he's trying to say it
in Spanish:
Tarde.

Tardy! he says.
Tar-day!
And then: *Detention!*

A Good Kid

My mother
is an engine,
always running.

She cooks
our dinner.
She brings it
to the table.
She spoons it out.
Night after night.

I don't understand,
she says
when I tell her
about my detention.
You're a good kid.
You never
get in trouble.

She presses
her fists
into her lower back.
She makes a face
like she's holding in
a sigh.

I look down
at the detention slip
in my hands.
I think
about how
detention
is for people
who can afford it.

People who can
miss the bus.

People whose mothers
don't come home
tired
from cleaning up
other people's messes.
And then
have to worry
about cleaning up
their own.

The Story I've Never Been Told

Sometimes,
when my mother
comes into my room
to kiss me
good night,
she sits
on the edge of the bed
and sighs.

Her gaze
goes
feather soft.
Her fingers
touch my cheek.
She whispers,
*You look
just like your father.*

Always,
I hold my breath,
hoping for more.

But there's
never any more.

My mother
has never told me
the story
of my father.
But her lips
press together
when she mentions him.
Her breath
catches
in her throat.
Her eyes
turn to glass.
And I can tell
he was
no knight
in shining armor.

When she kisses me
good night,
she tucks
a
strand
of
hair
behind my ear
and sighs.

And in the
space
of that sigh
there's a
whole story:

57

A girl in love.
A wisp
of hope.
A broken heart.

But there's also
my mother's love
for me.
And her
determination
to see
my story
turn out
differently.

The same
determination
our ancestors
had.

The same fire
that carried her
here,
all the way
from Guatemala.

Lucky

At lunchtime,
Andres sits on the grass.
He watches Brian Davis
throw a softball
several feet
away.

A fly
wanders too close
to my yogurt cup.
I
shoo
it away
with a scowl.

It's not the detention
that bothers me,
I tell Andres.
It's the way I got it.

Andres makes a sound
halfway
between a hum
and a sigh.
I lift my head
and see his eyes
following the arc
of Brian's throw.

59

Andres looks at me,
one thin, dark eyebrow
raised.

*You're just lucky your mom
didn't freak out,* he says.

I think of Andres's mom.
Her easy smile.
Her kind face.
Her laughing eyes.

*Your mom wouldn't
freak out,*
I tell him.

Andres makes a sound
halfway
between a cough
and a sigh.
*I have no idea
what my mother would do,*
he says.

Then he lies back
and closes his eyes.

Opening Credits

I saw a movie once.
Five high school students
served a Saturday detention.

At first,
they didn't get along.

But then
they started to talk.

They opened up
like blooming flowers.

They became friends.

In real life,
there are eight of us
serving detention.
We're sitting
as   far   apart
as we can.

I pull out
my sketchbook.

I open it
to a clean
white
page.

My pencil hovers
like a bumblebee
skimming over the petals
of a flower.

And then,
like curtains
falling open,
Josh Williams
walks in.

I stare
as he hands in
his detention slip.

My heart skips
with quiet excitement.
The way it always does
at the start of a movie.

Josh Williams

When he talks,
it's like
there's a joke
between us
that only he knows.

But I get the feeling
that if I talk to him
long enough,
he'll share the punchline
with me.

He'll let me in
on the secret.

He'll let me in.

Guatemalan Artists

Josh calls me Frida,
again.
When I tell him
Frida Kahlo
was Mexican,
he asks,
Aren't you Mexican?

A familiar anger
stirs
in my chest.

I was born here,
I snap.
*But my mother
is from
Guatemala.*

Josh looks at me
like he's trying to solve
a math problem.

But then his eyes
light up.
He smiles.

So,
tell me some
Guatemalan artists,
he says.

I open my mouth
to answer him.
But then I close it again.
Because I realize
I have no idea.

In the Car

My mother's hands
on the wheel
are dry and chapped.

Her face
is a map of lines.

Her eyes are bees
darting back and forth
between me
and the road.

I expect her to be angry
because she had to pick me up
from detention.
But when she looks at me,
her face isn't hard edges
and sharp corners.

It's soft lines.
It's wide circles.

Your grandmother called,
my mother says.
*She wants to know
if you read her letter.*

I turn my head
and stare
out the window.

I want to be angry
at my grandmother.
I want to be bitter.
I want to be indifferent.
And I am all those things.

But I'm also
something else.
Something that feels too much
like excited
by my grandmother's
sudden interest.

So I don't say anything.
I look at the trees.
I look at the sky.
I look anywhere
but at my mother's round,
worried face.

Lacrosse Practice

I was wondering,
I ask
my mother,
*if I could stay
after school
one day
and watch
lacrosse practice.*

My mother
frowns
at me
like I'm about
to do something
she doesn't like.

It's not right,
she tells me,
*to stand around
and make eyes at boys.
And, anyway,
you can't miss
the school bus.*

I pack
all the words
I want to say—

I'm not making eyes
at boys.
It's just
lacrosse practice.
Why
can't you ever
let me do
anything?—
into one
long
      and
           heavy
                sigh.

A Secret

When I was ten years old
my mother
told me not to
ride my bike
across the busy street.
The one that borders
our tiny neighborhood.

For a long time, it was enough
to ride my bike
right
up
to
the
edge
of my known world.
To turn around.
To come back home.

But, one day, I grew bored
with the
same
slow
circles.

That day, I rode my bike
right up

to
the
corner
where the cars zipped by
like lightning bolts.

I waited
for a lull in traffic.

I counted to three
in my head.

And then I pushed
away
from
the
curb,
my heart beating like thunder.

I made it to the other side.
And then
I made it back again.

And when I came home that night,
I had my
very
first
secret.
It was shining in my heart
like a diamond.

71

Four

For years,
it was
Gemma and Andres and me.
We sat in the grass
together
at lunch.
We sprinkled
Spanish
into our conversations
like a secret code.

Then,
Gemma was gone.
And it was just
me and Andres,
knocking
against each other.
Like boats
tied to a dock
and left
behind.

But today,
Josh wanders up
with Brian Davis.
The two of them
sit down
on the grass
with me and Andres.

Like it's the easiest thing
in the world.

And,
just like that,
there are four of us.

73

Blushing

I look
at Andres
and see his face
is flushed
bright red.

I look down at my hands
and wonder why
he's blushing.

I wonder if I'm
blushing,
too.

Marimba

My mother is standing
at the kitchen sink.
Her hands are sunk
up to the elbows
in soapy dishwater.

Her hips
       are swaying.

Her feet
       are tapping.

She's humming along
to the marimba music
streaming
through the living room speakers.

The marimba
is the national instrument
of Guatemala.

It's like a xylophone.
But it's so big,
sometimes you need more than one person
just to play one song.

Notes
      trip
and
      dance

across the kitchen.

Like a
      stream
of
      running
water.

Like
      wind chimes
in
      a summer
breeze.

Like
      a
drumming
      heart.

I like the songs
that sound like
twinkling lights.
The happy songs
that are like a
celebration.

But my mother's favorite
is "Luna de Xelajú."
A song about standing
in the moonlight
and missing
someone
you love.

My mother is standing
at the kitchen sink.
She's running a soapy sponge
over the dishes.

But her eyes
          are staring out the window.

Her eyes
          are gazing at the night sky.
          At the moon shining overhead.

The same moon
that shines over all of us.

The same moon
that hangs over everyone
she left behind in
Guatemala.

77

Popol Vuh

Sometimes
when I can't sleep,
my mother
tells me stories
from mythology.

These are not the stories
we learn in school.
They are not about
Greek gods
and Mount Olympus.

These are Mayan stories.
These are stories
from the *Popol Vuh*.
The sacred book
of the Mayan people.
Stories written
long before Columbus
sailed across the ocean.

In these stories,
the hero always wins
by being
smart
and brave.

But,
most importantly,
the hero wins
by making some sort of
sacrifice.

79

Butterflies

Andres's body
sits
in Gemma's chair.
But
his hands
dance in the air
between us
like birds.

Words are
falling
from
his
mouth.
But I only
catch
a few of them.

It's hard to hear
over the
whirlwind
of
butterflies
beating
nervous wings
against my heart.

When Josh walks into the room,
the butterflies settle.
Everything
goes still
inside me.
I don't even notice
when Andres
stops talking.

Lacrosse

The lacrosse field
is a sea
of green,
with goals
on either end.

Players dot the field
like pebbles.

Josh is there,
tall and smiling
in his pale blue jersey.

I watch him run
across the field.
I watch him run
back again.

Yes

The school buses
stand in a line,
mustard yellow
under the afternoon sun.

I know
I can't
miss the bus.

But
I don't want to leave
the edge
of the lacrosse field
just yet.

Andres wanders up.

He stands
beside me,
hands on his hips.

We could stay, he says.
We could watch
lacrosse practice.
My mom
could drive you home.

83

One by one,
the school buses
start
pulling
away
from the curb.

The sound
reminds me of
busy intersections.
Tiny neighborhoods.
Streets that mark
the edge
of a known world.

I look at Andres
and hold my breath.
I bite my lip.
I count to three.

And then I push
away
from the edge
of the field.
Away
from the school buses.
Toward
the white nets
where the players
are milling about.

I look back
over my shoulder
and smile at Andres.
I nod my head
and tell him,
Yes.

85

Anywhere

My sketchbook sits open
on my lap
as I watch the players
gallop
          back
and
          forth
across the field.

Andres is sitting
next to me.
But his eyes are pinned
to the players.

So I watch
them,
too.

I catch a glimpse
of Josh
diving
for the ball.

He moves
like a
          shooting
                    star.

Or
        a
                hummingbird.

He moves
the way watercolors
bleed
        across
                a page.

He races
        across
                the field.

Like he could go
anywhere
his legs carried him.

Anywhere
he wanted.

Anywhere
        at
                all.

To Just Be

When practice is finished,
Josh walks over.

He sits down
and asks,
Did you draw me?

I look down
at my open sketchbook.
At the empty page,
still untouched.

*It was all
so fast,*
I say.

That's what I like about it,
he tells me.
*There's no time
to think.*

He pushes back his hair
and I see his gray eyes,
shining bright
with laughter.

I wonder
what it would be like
to stop thinking.
To just run.
To just be.

Question

Josh smiles
like Christmas lights
strung unevenly.

*Do you want
to hang out
sometime?*
he asks.
Maybe this weekend?

The question comes
so fast,
there's no time
to think.

My stomach
does something
that reminds me of
roller coasters
and trampolines.

I hear myself say,
Okay.

Even though
I've never been
on a date before.

Even though
I've never been
asked.

Even though
I already know
what my mother
will say.

I look at Josh.
I look at my hands.
I look at the clean white page
on my lap.

I wonder
if this is what it's like
to run so fast
there's no time to think.

Ice

My heart is so light
that I float
into the house
like a figure skater
gliding
across the ice.

But when I see
my mother,
my happiness
melts
out from under me.

A Lie

Where have you been?
my mother cries.

I look
at the shadows
beneath her eyes.
At the lines
on her forehead.
At the threads of gray
in her dark hair.

I could tell her
the truth.

I *should*
tell her
the truth.

But I know
what she'll tell me.
I know
she'll be worried.
I know
she'll be scared.

93

So,
I take
a deep breath,
and I tell her
a lie.

*I missed my bus
because my locker
was broken.*

The lie
feels clunky
on my tongue.
Like shoes
that don't
quite fit.
And I can tell
by the stillness
in my mother's face
and the crease
between her brows
that she doesn't
believe me,
either.

Asleep

That night,
when my mother
kisses
me good night,
she doesn't
brush my hair
back
from my face.
Or say
soft words.
Or smile.

She sits
on the edge
of my bed,
as still
as a shadow.
Her brown hands
are quietly folded
in her lap.

*I don't know
what's going on
with you,*
she whispers.
*You don't get detentions.
You don't tell lies.
This is not who you are.*

Maya,
my mother says.
Talk to me.

But
I don't know
what to say.

So
I close my eyes.
I breathe in and out.
I pretend to be asleep.

And after a while,
my mother
stands up
and very slowly
walks away.

A New Day

I wake up
to the smells
of
cooking oil
and onions
and garlic.

I open my eyes
and the sun
is much too bright.
Like it is
on Saturday morning.

*Why didn't my alarm
go off?*
I wonder.
*Did I miss
the bus?
Am I
going to be late
for school?*

I find my mother
in the kitchen,
making breakfast.

She
should be
at work.

*I'm driving you
to school,*
she tells me.
*And I'll pick you up,
too.
You don't
have to worry
about missing the bus
anymore.*

I stand there,
sleepy eyed.
I try to think
of something
to say.

But I can't think
past the smell
of tortillas
scorching
on the hot stove.

Glass

When my mother
talks about
Guatemala,
she describes
a country
bordered
by wilderness.
Ringed
with volcanoes.
Peppered
with stone ruins.

But my world
is different.

My world is sidewalks
and trimmed hedges.
Clipped branches.
Clipped wings.

The only ruins
I've ever seen
were bits
of pottery
stored
safely
behind a glass case
in an air-conditioned museum.

99

I think
about those
broken shards
on the way to school.

I wonder
if that's what my mother
wants
for me.
To be stored away,
safe and sound
behind glass,
where nothing
can ever happen
to me.

Where
no one
can ever
touch me.

Circles

Walking past
my broken locker,
I hear
the sound
of Hailey Miller's
laughter.

I turn around
and catch her eye.
And my whole body
goes
still.

When we were
in third grade,
it rained
for a week.
The playground
turned muddy.
The fields
behind the school
flooded.
Our teacher sat us
on the floor
and pulled out
a big jar
of marbles.

The goal,
she explained,
is to knock
all the other marbles
out
of the circle.

I watch,
now,
as Hailey Miller
ducks her head
and whispers
to the closed ring
of her friends.
And all
I can think about
is my third-grade teacher.
And all
those marbles
getting knocked out
one
by
one.

Unsaid

Josh
is waiting
for me
outside
of math class,
and my heart
bounces
like a kite
at the sight of him.

Are we still on
for this weekend?
he asks me.

I open my mouth
to tell him
about
my mother.
About how
she wouldn't let me
stay after school
to watch
lacrosse practice.
How she won't let me
ride the bus
anymore.
How there's no way
she'd ever let me go
on a date.

But
the words
get lost
somewhere
between my head
and my mouth.

Because:
What if
I tell him,
and he thinks
I'm making up
excuses?
What if
he thinks
I don't like him?
What if
he decides
he doesn't like
me?

Give me your phone,
Josh says.
I'll put in my number.

I don't want to tell him
I'm the only person in this school
who doesn't have
her own phone.
So I mutter something
about leaving my phone at home
and give him our house number instead.

I'll call you,
Josh says.

I close
my eyes
and take
a deep breath.
I pretend
I'm someone else.
Someone
who doesn't have to
make excuses.
Someone
whose mother
doesn't keep her
locked up
in a glass box.

Josh asks
if everything is okay.
And because
I'm someone else
for a while,
I smile.
And I nod.
And I say,
Yes.

The Space Between Spaces

When I was little,
it was always
me and my mom.

I was like the sun,
and she spun
around me
constant and close.

I never knew
we were missing
anything.

Until one day
I did.

And then
all I could see
was the way bodies
were made with
two
hands
to be held.

All I could see
was the way
other kids
drew their families with
two
smiling grown-ups.
And the way
I drew my family
with only
one.

107

Things I Can't Say

*Gemma says
you haven't called her.*

Andres's face
is scrunched up
in a frown.
He's looking
at me
like he did
in seventh grade
when I hid
his pencil sharpener
and wouldn't
give it back.

I turn and look
at the classroom door.
At the kids
trickling in
like water
dripping
from a faucet.

I wonder why
Gemma
is complaining to Andres
when she's supposed to be
my best friend?

Maybe
we should do something
Saturday,
Andres says.
Just the three of us.

I shake
my head.

I want
to tell him
I have a date
on Saturday.

I want
to call Gemma
and tell her,
too.

I want
it
so
much,
the words
are like a hot-air balloon
inside me.

But
I force myself
to stay quiet.

I hold
my breath.

I hold
my heart.

Because without
my mother's
permission,
I have no idea
how
I'm going to make
my first date
happen.

Talk to Me

At the dinner table,
I cut my *chile relleno*
right
down
the
middle.

Rice and tomato
fall out
of their bell pepper cage.
Like secrets
spilling out
of a broken heart.

Talk to me,
my mother says.
I picture myself
opening my mouth
and telling her
about Josh.
About Saturday.
About our date ...

But the word
date
catches
like a tomato seed
between my teeth.

117

And I realize
I can't
tell my mother
any of it.

Lines

My mother
      is a collection
      of lines.

The lines of gray
      in her dark hair
      are like threads
      of light.

The lines near her mouth
      are sharp
      and straight.

The lines around her eyes
      are softer.
      More delicate.
      Like the thin ghosts
      of her laughter.

My mother
      is a collection
      of lines.

Family lines.

Bloodlines.

Lines that used to
        tie us together.

Lines that have been
        erased
        by time.

Ten Cuidado

Ten cuidado,
my mother always
tells me
as I'm walking
out the door.

Be careful.

I think of
the broken shards
of pottery.
The ones we saw,
once,
at the museum.
I wonder
if that's what happens
when you're not careful.

I Just Want to Be Free

Sometimes
when I'm on my bike,
I pedal as hard
and as fast as I can.

I pretend I'm a bird.
I pretend I'm a shooting arrow.

I pretend I'm free.

Iron Door

Your grandmother
called again,
my mother tells me,
interrupting my thoughts.

She looks at me
closely,
waiting
for my reaction.

But what I feel
is too big.
Too much.
Too scary
to be said
out loud.

So,
I hold my mouth
closed
like an iron door
and say
nothing.

The Ghost

People say
you can't
miss
what you
never had.
And for a long time
that was true.

But, lately,
when my mother and I
are sitting
at the dinner table,
I think of
my grandmother's letter.
I imagine
a ghost
sitting with us.

The ghost
is the story
of my father.

The ghost
is the story
I've never been told.

The ghost
is an absence
where a presence
should be.

In the Dark

When my mother comes
into my room
to say
good night,
she sits
on the edge
of my bed.
She takes
a deep breath
like she's about to dive
underwater.

*I can tell
something
isn't right,*
she says.

In the gentle
cover
of darkness,
words
spring
to my lips
like startled birds.

But I press
my mouth closed.

I lock
them in.

In the silence
that follows,
my heart
is like a bell
ringing
please
      please
            please ...

But
I don't know
what I'm asking for.
And my mother
only
sighs.

Phone Call

The next morning,
my mother
is in the kitchen.

Her back
is to me.

Her shoulders
are hunched.

She's talking on the phone.
But her voice is hushed.
And I can tell by the way
she grips the counter
that it's not
a happy call.

When she hangs up,
she turns around.
She looks at me
with sad eyes.

That was for you,
she tells me.

I frown,
wondering if it was
Gemma.
Or Andres.
Or even
my grandmother.

But then
my mother says,
*He said his name was
Josh.
He called to ask
about your date
on Saturday.*

I stand perfectly still.
A statue.
A stone ruin.

What did you tell him?
I whisper.

My mother
shakes her head.

*I told him my daughter
would never make a date
without asking me first.*

But I can tell
by the way
her mouth
pulls down
at the edges
that she knows
it's exactly what
her daughter
has done.

A Piece of Paper

I stand
in the middle
of my room.
I am as helpless
as an autumn tree
whose leaves
are
       falling
           away.

I want
to dive
under the covers.

I want
to disappear.

I want
to cry.

But something
catches
my eye
as I head for my bed.
A piece of paper
on my nightstand.

A crinkled white scrap
that's been
smoothed out
but doesn't
quite
        lay
            flat.

My Grandmother's Letter

I recognize
my grandmother's letter,
and I realize
my mother
must have found it
in the kitchen trash.

I pick it up
with shaking hands.
I hold it up
to
     the
         light.

Querida Maya,
the letter says.

My first instinct
is to crumple it up
once more.

But then
I think of my mother.
I think of the way
she sits
on the edge
of my bed

127

each night,
a story locked
inside her heart.

I look down
at my grandmother's
letter.
At the words
that bleed
across
   the
      page.

The letter is short.
No more than
two paragraphs.

But when
I'm done reading,
I realize
two paragraphs
are all it takes
to take a heart
and
   break
      it.

A Bad Idea

I hold
my grandmother's letter
between
me
and
my mother
like a wall.

My mother
is watching me
like I'm a glass
of water
balanced
on the edge
of a counter.

I skim down
until I find
the words
I'm looking for.
And then I read them
to her
out loud:

I've talked to your mother
about sending you
to Guatemala.

*She thinks it might be
a good idea.*

I hold the letter
away from me.
As if the words
could find their way
off the page
and onto my skin.

Maybe

My mother is quiet
for a very long time.
She looks
at the floor.
She looks
at the wall.
She looks
at the window,
with its view
of the moon.

And then
she turns
back to me.
She takes
a deep breath.

You're growing up,
she says.

I can feel you
pulling away.

Already,
your heart
is someplace else.
Somewhere I can't reach.

131

And it scares me.

Maybe,
in Guatemala,
you can slow down.

Maybe
you can learn
about your past.
About
your ancestors.

Maybe
you can figure out
who you are
and who
you
want to be.

What I (Don't) Say

I try
to picture myself
in Guatemala.
Far away
        from my friends.
Far away
        from Josh.
Far away
        from everything I know.

I open
my mouth
to tell my mother
I don't want to
go.
But tears
scratch
the back
of my throat.
So I snap
my mouth
closed.

I put
my grandmother's letter
down
on the counter.
I shake my head.
I turn away.

What does it matter,
anyway,
what I say?

How could it matter,
now,
when it never
mattered
before?

Words

My mother's words
sit in my gut
all day.
Like a stone.
Like a piece of flint.

They flash
before me
like neon signs
lighting up
everything
that's gone wrong.
Leaving
nowhere
for me to hide.

Escape

After school,
I try to do my homework.
But I can't sit still.
I can't think.
So
I grab my sweater
and head for the door.

My mother
calls out
to let me know
dinner is ready.

But I can't stop
my feet
from moving.

I can't stop
my heart
from hurting.

Away

I ride my bike
away
from our house.

I ride across
the busy intersection
that used to be
the edge
of my world.

I ride past
the museum
with its pottery
in glass cases.

And when I look up,
I realize
I've ridden my bike
all the way
to Gemma's house.

And something inside me
finally cracks
and gives way.

Echoes

Gemma's house
has the highest ceilings
of any house
I've ever seen.
If you walk
across the hardwood floor
in anything
but bare feet,
your footsteps
echo
echo
echo
in your ears.

I sit in Gemma's room,
my face sticky
with sweat.

I try
not to look
at the neat stack
of folded laundry
on her dresser.

I try
not to picture
my mother gently setting
the clean clothes down.

138

Or moving
across the room
to make Gemma's bed.

I open my mouth
and all my secrets
spill out.

I tell Gemma
everything.
Everything
        I've held in.
Everything
        she's missed.

My words
echo
echo
echo
in the giant space
between us.
And when I finish talking,
I look up
and see Gemma's face
has turned the color
of fresh strawberries.
Like it does
when she sits
for too long
under the sun.

139

Racing

When we were nine,
Gemma and I
climbed up
to the top
of the sledding hill,
our breath
loud
in our ears.

We stood
at the very top,
our hands held tight,
and counted down
from three.

Then we ran
          down
              the hill.

At first,
it was exciting.

Gravity snatched me up,
pulling me
faster
and
faster.

Until it felt like my legs
weren't my own.

But halfway down,
Gemma started falling behind.

So, I opened my hand.
I let go.

When I reached the bottom
I fell into a heap,
laughing and gasping.

I lay on my back
and waited for Gemma
to fall on the grass
beside me.

I waited and waited.
But Gemma never came.
And when I finally sat up,
I found her sitting
halfway up the hill,
all alone
and crying.

Gemma

Gemma sits
at the other end
of her room.
Her eyes are as wide
as they were
that day
on the hill
when I left her
behind.

What's wrong?
I ask her.

Gemma doesn't say
anything
for a while.
And the longer
she is quiet,
the more my heart beats
and drums
like it's trying to run away.

But I sit still.
I stay.

And, finally,
Gemma says,

142

I haven't made any friends
at my new school.
Everybody else
has been
together
since the first grade.
I'm
the outsider.
The newcomer.
I don't fit in.

I look
at Gemma.
She's so perfect
in my eyes.
How could anyone
not want
to be
her friend?

Why didn't
you tell me?
I ask.

Because
you haven't been there!
she cries.
You never call!
And when I call you,
all you want
to talk about
is Josh.

143

I think
of the last time
I talked to Gemma.
How I sat
in the kitchen.
How my fingers
picked out her phone number.
How I didn't
even wait
for her to say
hello
before I dove
into my own story.

It feels like ages ago.

I pinch my lips shut
and look down
at the floor.

I'm sorry,
I say.

I Think

I think I got caught up
in the way it feels
to let go.
To be someone else
for a while.

I think
I messed up.

I think I forgot
that letting go
doesn't have to mean
leaving others
behind.

Circles and Squares

Gemma and I
lie on the floor
of her room
and stare up
at her white ceiling.

She tells me
about private school
and how
she doesn't fit in.
How she feels
like a square
in an ocean
of circles.

Like a red marble,
I say,
mixed in
with the blue ones.

Exactly!
Gemma cries.

And,
for the first time
that night,

I hear the hint
of a smile
in her voice.

We lie
on the floor
of her bedroom.
Two girls
floating
on a soft
cream
carpet.

Gemma is quiet
for a very
long
time.
And just when I think
she's not going to say
anything,
I feel her fingers
brush mine.

I've missed you,
she tells me.

And then
she says,
Thank you.

For what?
I ask.

She turns her head
and looks at me.
For listening,
she says.

Her eyes
shimmer
in the soft glow
from her desk lamp,
like a light
at the end
of a
very
long
tunnel.

Listen

All the way home,
I think of Gemma.

I think of
everything
that was going on
inside her.
A whole world
I didn't know about
because I wasn't there.
I wasn't listening.

I wonder
if everyone
has a world like that
inside them.

I wonder
what that world
looks like.

I wonder
what I'd hear
if I pressed my ear
to their hearts.

All the way home
my heart knocks
against my chest
like a message
written in Morse code.

I hold my breath
and listen.

Family Tree

In fourth grade
we drew our
family trees.
Our teacher
pinned them up
on the bulletin board
outside our classroom.

After school,
I walked down the hall
and looked
at all the trees.

Every tree
had snaking branches
extending out
in both directions.

But my tree
was lopsided.

My tree
only stemmed
and rooted
on one side.
My mother's side.

151

It's not fair,
I complained to my mother.
It's so different.
It's so ugly.

My mother
looked at me
and sighed.

Yes,
she said.
It's different.
But, sometimes,
things that are
different
are more beautiful
because of their differences.

Locked Doors

I spin the lock
in both directions.
But my locker
still
       won't
open.

Who I Am

Hailey Miller
makes an impatient noise
behind me.

I can't get to my locker,
she snaps,
if you're standing
in

        my
way.

I move aside
and mumble an apology.
But she only frowns.

Aren't you the girl,
she asks,
whose mother
cleans Brian Davis's house?

My heart starts to sink
under the weight
of her friends' laughter.
But then I catch
Hailey Miller's eye.

I think of
what
she sees
when she looks
at me.
Brown skin.
Plain clothes.
A mother
who cleans
other people's houses.

And then I think of
what
she *doesn't* see
because
she's not
paying attention.
My sketches.
My dreams.
A mother
who was brave enough
to come here
from Guatemala.

A mother
who was strong enough
to stay.

Hailey's question rings in my ears.
Aren't you the girl
whose mother
cleans Brian Davis's house?

155

She wants me
to be ashamed.

She wants me
to be embarrassed
because
I
              am
different.

But I think
of my mother.

I think of
what she said to me
about things
that are different.

I lift my chin
and look Hailey
in the eye.

I nod my head and I say,
Yes, I am.

I Wonder

I wonder what the world
inside Hailey Miller
looks like.

I wonder if I'll
ever
know.

I wonder if she ever
lets anyone
close enough
to listen.

All I know for sure
is that I'm finally going to
request a locker
that isn't broken.

Something Important

When I walk
into homeroom,
Andres
is already there,
sitting in the seat
that used to be
Gemma's.

I slide in next to him
and take a deep breath.

I want to tell Andres
about how
I missed
my first date
with Josh.
About my mother's plans
to send me
to Guatemala.
About Gemma …

But instead,
I think of
hidden worlds.
I bite my lip.
I count to ten.

I look at Andres,
sitting with his hands
folded
and his head
down.

Hey, I whisper,
How was your weekend?

Andres
looks up.
He lifts
one dark eyebrow.
He tips his head
to one side
like he's trying to decide
something important.

Then he leans toward me
and sighs.

The World Inside Andres

Between classes,
Andres and I
sit on the grass
in front of the school
and he tells me
about the world
inside him.

He tells me
about his crush
on Brian Davis.

He has never
said anything
about Brian
before today.
But
if I'd been
paying attention,
I would
have noticed.

I would have seen
how Andres looks
whenever Brian
is near.

It's the same way
I look
whenever
I'm with Josh.

I've been so scared,
Andres tells me,
that my mother
will find out.
So scared
of what she'll do.
So scared
of what she'll say.

I think of
Andres's mother.
Her easy smile.
Her kind face.
Her laughing eyes.

I think
I understand
a part
of what Andres feels.
I've been afraid
to tell
my own mother
anything.
I've been afraid
to let her into the world
inside me.
I've been afraid ...

I don't know
what your mother
will say
if you tell her.
But whatever happens,
you're not alone.
I'm here,
I tell Andres.

Andres smiles.
And I realize
it's the first time
he's done that
in a really long time.

Explanations

Josh doesn't show up
for homeroom.

He isn't waiting for me
outside of math class.

I don't see him
in the halls.

At lunch,
it's just
me and Andres,
sitting by ourselves on the grass.

I guess
I'd be pretty angry, too,
Andres tells me.
You kind of stood him up.

I didn't stand him up,
I grumble.
I just...

You just what?
Andres prods.

163

But I only
shake my head.

I want
to tell Andres
I was
afraid
Josh
wouldn't like me.

Afraid
he'd be angry.

Afraid
he would see me—
really see me—
and turn away
from what he saw.

But Andres
isn't the person
who needs to hear
my explanations.

Is It Josh?

Where are you going?
Andres asks
as I gather up
my empty yogurt cup.

*I have to find
someone,*
I tell him.

Is it Josh?
he asks.
There's a teasing whine
in his voice
that makes
my face
feel all hot.

I wipe at the grass stains
on my knees.

I smile at Andres.

The Lacrosse Field

The lacrosse field
is a sea of green.
An empty ocean.
Except for
one figure
standing in
the center
like a lost ship.

Apology

Josh stands
on the grass,
his lacrosse stick
slung
across his shoulders.
He watches me
walk toward him.

I wish
I had more
to give him
than words.

But all I can do
is walk up to him,
empty-handed.

All I can do
is look him
in the eye.

All I can do
is say,
I'm sorry.

Understanding

I don't understand,
Josh says.
Why
did you say
you'd meet me
on Saturday?

I tell him
I was afraid.
He makes a sound
that's halfway between
a laugh
and a groan.

Afraid of what?
he asks.

I shrug
one shoulder
and sigh.
Afraid
you wouldn't like me
anymore
if you knew
who I really was.

I tell him about
my mother.
How she came
from Guatemala
before I was born.

I tell him about
my father.
How he left her
all alone.

I tell him about
how my mother
is always saying,
It's not safe.
You're too young.
Todo en su tiempo.

And when
I'm finished,
Josh says,
I would have understood.

I Know

I know
I made a mistake.

I know
I ruined things.

I know
I can't go back
and make it right.

Walking Away

The bell rings,
warning us
we're late for class.

Josh drops
his lacrosse stick
to his side.

He turns
and starts to walk
away.

But after
a few steps,
he stops.

Come on,
he says.
I'll walk you to class.

177

Everything
In Between

A teacher once asked Gemma
if her parents were European
because her skin
is the color of marshmallows
before they've been toasted.

People think anyone
who speaks Spanish
should be brown.
Like me.

They don't realize
we are a rainbow of words.
Of dialects.
Of accents.

They don't realize
Latino
can mean white.
Or brown.
Or black.
Or anything in between.

A Girl

In art class,
I walk over
to the window
and look at my reflection
on the window pane.

I lean in close
and study the girl
in front of me.

Brown eyes,
like tamarind pods.

Brown hair,
like turning leaves.

Skin the color of
dulce de leche.

Or beach sand.

Or a warm mug
of hot chocolate
in the middle
of winter.

173

I add myself
to the picture
I started.
The picture of Gemma,
smiling
under the summer sun.

I add myself in,
bit by bit.

It's not even close
to a masterpiece.
But it's a good start,
for now.

Let Me In

My mother
and
I
sit
at the dinner table,
as silent
as undercurrents.

I can feel
her
studying me
like I'm a painting.
Like I'm a sketch
of someone
she used to know.

Talk to me,
my mother says.

The words
swim
inside me.
A whole world
of them.
But I don't know
how
to let
them out.

I don't know how
to let her in.

I think of
Andres
and his crush
on Brian.

I think of
untold stories.

I think of
Gemma.
How
I didn't know
what was going on with her
until I listened.

But,
also,
how she had to find
the words
to tell me.

How she had to
let me in.

The Ocean

There is an ocean
between
my mother
and
me.
There is no way
to swim across it.

I open my mouth,
even though
my heart
is pounding.

*I don't want
to go
to Guatemala,*
I say.

And then
I snap
my mouth
closed
like a gate.

I sit very
still.

I wait
for my mother
to tell me
all the reasons
I have to go.
All the reasons
I can't stay here.
All the ways
I've got it
wrong.

But my mother
only
puts her fork
down.

Choices

I came
to this country,
my mother says,
because
your father
wanted to.

But
I stayed
because
it was a land
of freedom.
A land
of choices.

The word
choices
makes my heart
beat
like a bird
about to take
flight.

I'd like to go
to Guatemala,
someday,
I say.

But not
with
my grandmother.

I look up
at my mother.
At her tired,
puffy eyes.
The soft lines
of her face.
The smooth skin
of her brow.

I'd like to go
to Guatemala,
someday,
I tell her.
But I want to go
with
you.

My mother closes
her eyes.
She nods
and sighs.
Her lips
form the faint shadow
of a smile.

The Ocean II

There is an ocean
between
me
and
my mother.
There is no way
to swim across it.

But maybe,
between the two of us,
we can start
to build
a bridge.

Stories

Sometimes,
when I can't sleep,
my mother tells me stories
from the *Popol Vuh*.

But, tonight,
I gather my courage.
Tonight, I ask my mother
to tell me
a different story.

Tonight, I ask about
my father.

My Mother's Story

I fell in love with your father,
my mother tells me,
because he had
big dreams.

His dreams
brought us here
all the way
from Guatemala.

But,
when we got here,
your father wasn't happy.
He wanted to keep moving.
He wanted to run.

There was a restlessness
inside your father
that no one
could still.
A restlessness
that no place
could silence.
Because the thing
he was trying to run away from
was himself.

183

In the end,
she tells me,
there wasn't
enough room
in your father's heart
for both
his restlessness
and his family.

So he made a choice.
He left us.
He chose
himself.

I lie very quietly
while my chest
fills up with sadness.

There was no room
for my mother
in my father's heart.

There was no room
for our family.

There was no room
for me.

My mother leans close.

184

She brushes my hair
gently back from my cheek.
She places a soft kiss
on my forehead
like she's planting a seed
in the soil.

But
I chose you,
Maya,
she says.

I chose
us.

She takes my hand
in hers
and holds it so tightly
I think she's
never
going to let it go.

But,
in the end,
she does.

How a Hero Wins

In the stories
from the *Popol Vuh*,
the hero wins
by being brave.
By making a sacrifice.

When,
at last,
I fall asleep,
I dream of a moon
hanging in the black sky.
It shines down
on everything
my mother left behind
in Guatemala.

I dream
of heroes.

I dream
of sacrifice.

I dream
of what it means
to win.

You Are Maya

My mother
doesn't think I'm ready
to go on a date
like other girls do.

*You are not
other girls,*
she tells me.
*You are Maya.
You have a whole life
ahead of you.*

Take it slow,
she tells me.
Take your time.

Todo en su tiempo.

187

Dinner

Tonight,
we are sitting
at the dinner table.
Just the
              three
              of
              us.
My mother.
Me.
And Josh.

My mother
keeps stealing
curious glances
and nodding to herself.
And I can tell that she approves
of this American boy
who is so careful
and polite
with his words.

After dinner,
I tell my mother that
Josh and I
are going
for a walk.

For a minute,
those words
hover
in the air
between
us.

(*It's not safe.*
You're too young.
Todo en *su tiempo.*)

But then
my mother smiles
at me.

Ten cuidado,
she tells me.
Be careful.

I give her
a quick hug.
I tell her
what I always
tell her.
I love you.

My mother
wraps her arms
around me
and holds me close.

189

I love you, too,
she whispers.

And then she opens up her arms
like she's opening a cage.
And, with a sigh,
she
       lets
             me
                go.

WANT TO KEEP READING?

If you liked this book, check out another book
from West 44 Books:

ONLY PIECES
BY EDD TELLO

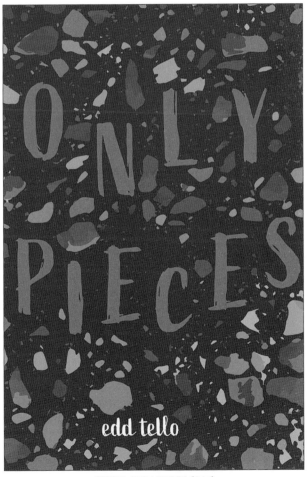

ISBN: 9781978596016

HOME

It's Saturday.
Seven a.m.

The first rays of sun
sweep through
the broken blinds
of our crummy apartment.

The phone rings.
Amá quickly gets up.

I lie in bed.
My eyes are red.
I didn't sleep well.

I manage to
go to the kitchen.

Amá is crying.
She covers her mouth.

I think it's Grandma
she's talking with.

She cries every time
they speak on the phone.

It's been five years
since Abuela last visited us.
We were living in Texas
back then.

But this time,
Amá's face
doesn't look sad.

She hangs up.

It was your father.
He's coming home.

What?
I ask.
Just to make sure
I heard it right.

He's in Bakersfield, mijo.
We will pick him up.
Hurry.
Put some shoes on.

I puff out my chest
and put some jeans on
that my dad gave me
two birthdays ago.

I take
my writing journal
I left
on the floor last night.

Amá washes her face
and mops the floor
a little bit.
She's ready in 10.

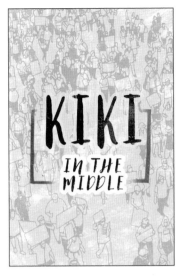

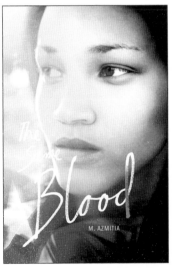

CHECK OUT MORE BOOKS AT:
www.west44books.com

An imprint of Enslow Publishing

WEST 44 BOOKS™

About The Author

Claudia is a Miami native who currently resides in
Western New York. Her work has appeared in
Fun 4 Kids in Buffalo and *Woo! Jr.*, and in the online
journal *Touch: The Journal of Healing*. She is a first
generation Guatemalan American. When not writing,
she is either playing in the snow with her husband
and son, or flying through the air on a trapeze.